GNOME
WAY OUT

A TALE OF MURDER AND REVENGE
BY VINCE FONT

Published by Glass Spider Publishing
www.glassspiderpublishing.com

ISBN 978-0-692-34363-0
Cover design by Jane Font
Edited by Nancy LaFever

To Daisy Jane, my biggest and bestest fan, who I would never kill and bury in the back yard.

The scream exploded from Henry Keller's lips with the force of a freight train horn at close range. He swung the meat hammer, clipping the tip of Vicky's forehead and decorating the kitchen cabinets with a fine red mist. She reeled violently and crashed against the stack of piled dishes in the sink.

If she'd fallen, she might have lived. As crazy as Henry was, he hadn't set out to murder his wife that night, and the sight of her decked out on the puke-yellow linoleum might have been enough to satisfy his rage. But instead of giving him what he wanted, she remained upright. She didn't even scream. Only turned her bloodied face to him and spat.

"Is that the best you can do?" she hissed.

Clutching at the gouge in her forehead, Vicky reached behind her and grabbed the first thing her hand fell upon. It was the ceramic coffee mug she'd bought him for their second anniversary, the one with the words *Masculine Mug* emblazoned across it in caveman font.

Below that was the cartoonish caricature of a rabbit perched atop a treasure chest, and the obligatory punchline: *With a little hare on its chest.* Henry had hated it. The knowledge had given Vicky a secret smile.

She curled her fingers around the mug and brought it fast against his right cheek. But rather than the payoff she anticipated, it only bounced off with a hollow *clunk*. She didn't even get the satisfaction of hearing Henry howl in pain. Before the mug hit the floor, he fired back with another blow. This time, the hammer penetrated Vicky's skull and she went down with the force of a body let loose from the gallows.

Dead.

Henry stood over his wife's corpse and watched the pool of blood spread around her head. The sweat attack that had sprung just seconds before he reached for the hammer finally stopped, its remnants congealing on his skin like a film of filth. He tossed the bloody tenderizer onto the kitchen counter and started for the bathroom but stopped when it occurred to him if he showered now, he'd only have to do it again later.

Stepping over Vicky's body, he crossed the kitchen and opened the door that connected to the garage. He stood in the threshold and thought of what to do next, chewing his lip in the manner Vicky had always hated. "You look like a camel when you do that," she'd told him once, laughing, but the backhand that came in response had shut her up good and ensured she never spoke of camels in his presence again.

The Oldsmobile in the garage had an enormous trunk. He could throw Vicky into it, drive out to a ravine in the middle of nowhere and dump her—but there was always a chance her body would be found. Once it had, there would be questions. Too many questions. There had to be a better way.

His eyes scanned the contents of the garage and landed on the wooden garden gnome perched atop a tiny workbench in the corner. Vicky had brought it in from the back yard the night before with the intent of adding a fresh layer of paint to its fading coat. She'd never get the chance now. He snickered at the thought. Then a light went on in his head.

There were at least a dozen others, maybe

more, scattered throughout the back yard. Vicky had loved those gnomes more than she had ever loved him, and through the years that love had developed into a perverse fixation—especially after Henry had let it slip, in a rare moment of candor, that he had been terrified of the things as a child.

It was a fear no more irrational than the fear of clowns or antique furniture, Henry knew this, and he was damned if he was going to let it get the best of him by asking Vicky to move on to something a bit more upscale and antiseptic, like pink flamingos. So he'd closed his mouth and kept it shut. The following day, Vicky had returned from an excursion to the local farmer's market with another half dozen of the little bastards.

Each had been artisan-sculpted and bore its own unique characteristics, which somehow made them more frightening than if they'd looked like generic assembly line clones. Some stood. Others sat. Some lay on their sides with legs crossed and pipes dangling lazily from their gobs, while still others held the tools of their imaginary trade in their small fat hands—a shovel here, a pickaxe there—like miniature humanoids suspended in motion at the start of some unenviable task. All wore long, flowing beards and mirthful expressions. And they had been the love of Vicky's pathetic life.

If she loved them so damn much, Henry thought, *why not bury her in the back yard where she can be closer to them?*

The tickle inside was too tangible to ignore. There was something about the idea so deliciously horrid, so undeniably poetic, that it actually caused him to laugh out loud.

Genius.

With a resolute nod, Henry closed the door to the garage. He hopped over the egg-shaped blood puddle that encircled Vicky's head and pulled open the sliding glass door that led out onto the cement pad of the back porch.

It was a small back yard, but private. A six-foot wooden fence barred the view of the neighbors on either side, aided by a dense grouping of maple trees that rendered all activity both inside and outside the home virtually invisible.

There was a padlocked tool shed in the far

corner of the yard that Henry had built himself. Lying in a direct path between the back porch and the shed was Vicky's garden—the place where she had tried and failed and tried again to draw life from the barren ground. Eventually, just like with everything else, she had thrown in the towel. Now it would be her grave.

Henry tramped over the dry cracked soil and fished a ring of keys from his pants pocket. He undid the padlock on the shed door and stepped inside. There was a short-handled shovel hanging from a rack on the wall above a flawlessly clean workbench. He pulled it down and walked back outside.

Working fast, he plowed a hole into the earth smack dab in the middle of the garden. He dug deep enough to keep the smell of rot from rising to the surface, but shallow enough so that he could dig it out in a hurry and move the body somewhere else if he had to. It was a contingency plan that seemed foolproof, and even though Henry was an absolute beginner, he reckoned he might be getting the hang of this.

When he decided the hole was deep enough, he put the shovel down and went back inside the house. Dragging Vicky's body out and throwing it into the ground would be easy—it was only a handful of short steps from the back door to the garden and the only real trouble he'd have would be making sure not to leave a snail trail of blood and brain matter behind—but he couldn't risk a nosy neighbor deciding to peek over the fence at just the wrong moment.

He could cut her into pieces in the bathtub and move her out of the house piecemeal. But that would require a lot more work than he was willing to put into it. Besides, the thought of sawing through bone and cartilage made him shudder.

I may have just killed my wife, he thought, *but I'm certainly no monster.*

Then he remembered the quilt, and a dark smile spread across his face. Vicky's mother, that despicable beast, had gifted it to them about five years ago, just before her own thankful death. Now that Vicky was out of the picture for good, the quilt would go with her.

Two birds, one hammer. Not bad for a first-timer.

He went into the bedroom and tore the quilt from the bed with one vicious tug. Pillows flew and knocked over the bedside lamp Vicky had always read by at night. Those tasteless sex books that passed for literature among the oversexed and undereducated. As he dragged the quilt behind him into the kitchen, he vowed to feed every single one of them to the paper shredder just as soon as she was in the ground.

Pushing the kitchen table aside, he spread the quilt on the linoleum next to Vicky's body. He used his feet to roll her onto it, delivering one last kick for good measure as he did. There was a loud crack as the vertebrae in her spine snapped, and he felt a sharp pain on the insole of his foot—but instead of reacting, he grimaced delightfully. Then he folded one end of the quilt over her body and rolled her up like a burrito.

He dragged the limp package outside, grinning at the wet smacking sound her skull made inside the quilt as it bounced against the cement pad.

When the grave was covered, Henry plunged the shovel into the ground and took stock of his surroundings. It was an especially noiseless night, the kind he preferred. Not a sound emanated from any of the surrounding homes, and even the worthless yapper that lived in the back yard two houses down had finally shut up for the night. The lack of light from all directions indicated his neighbors had long gone to bed, completely oblivious to the act he'd just committed or the fact he'd just transformed his back yard into an impromptu burial plot for one.

Committed.

He thought about the word as he paced the length of the garden, packing the earth under his heels. Just the sound of it tumbling around in his head felt oddly out of place. He didn't feel like he'd *committed* anything. Silencing Vicky once and for all had been an act more akin to an inspired performance than a crime.

The way she'd dropped under the force of that final blow, the way she had descended with such suddenness and finality, couldn't have been better executed if it had been choreographed. The blood that had pooled slowly around her pulverized head, its almost earthy hue contrasting sharply against the garish linoleum, had looked to his eyes like a work of art more striking than any Jackson Pollock splatter-job he'd ever seen. If he wasn't as smart as he was, he might even have taken a snapshot of the sight so he could remember it forever. But Henry wasn't stupid.

Methodically, he continued to pace, flattening the soil beneath his feet. Each step delivering him further from that dreadful old life with Vicky. An existence spent suffering her intolerable presence; tuning out her infantile attempts at intelligent conversation; listening to her caterwauling complaints anytime he exercised his right to lay hands on and lay hands off at will. Over, finally. Just like a bad movie.

When the ground was level, he took the shovel into the shed and polished it to an immaculate sheen. Then he returned it to its place on the rack, padlocked the door, and headed for the house.

He was halfway across the lawn when he caught sight something standing in the shadows.

It startled him to a full stop, his feet performing a clumsy, spontaneous tap dance before finally planting into place. As Henry's eyes adjusted to the darkness, the form began to take on a clear shape.

It was one of the garden gnomes. The one

with the periwinkle coat Vicky had always called "Perry" in those infuriating moments when she saw fit to actually speak to the damn things. Once, Henry had come into the back yard to find her having a full-fledged conversation with it. Her shamed reaction at being discovered had been priceless—invaluable enough for Henry to let the incident slide with no more than a contemptuous smirk—but apparently Vicky had been up to her old games as recently as today, because instead of being positioned at the head of the garden as it normally was, the gnome named Perry was now standing just outside the ring of light thrown from the kitchen window.

A shudder let loose from the base of Henry's spine and worked its way up his scalp like a snake. He fought against it like he always did whenever he caught himself staring too long at the garden gnomes. It was the eyes that did it, every goddamned time. Those painted pitch-black peepers that seemed to follow you until you were out of their line of sight. And now this, an oversight on his part that someone of a less practical mind would have taken as evidence the thing had moved on its own.

Of course it hadn't. Of course it had been there all along, put there by Vicky herself, probably in an attempt to scare the hell out of him. And of course, it had worked.

Approaching the garden gnome, Henry cocked his leg back at the knee and thrust his foot forward as hard as he could. Perry flew like a cannonball and bounced off the side of the house with an earsplitting crack as wooden fragments rained in all directions.

The payoff felt almost as good as killing Vicky had, but it was a stupid mistake. Two houses down, the neighborhood yapper flew into a fit of irate barking. Henry froze in place and closed his eyes, waiting for the inevitable—a nearby voice crying out in alarm; a flood of lights; the shriek of police sirens. When nothing came, he crept soundlessly inside.

After a full minute of unchecked cacophony, the ungodly mutt grew tired and closed its mouth. All was still and silent again.

Back in the house, Henry began the task of

cleaning up the bloody mess Vicky had left behind. Watching shows like *Dexter* and *Snapped* had taught him a lot about the mistakes amateur killers often made. Enough for him to know that simply blotting up the blood wouldn't do the trick. Not with all the gadgets and chemicals crime scene experts used these days. He had to be crafty if he wanted to get past this.

Luminol, that's what they called it. The chemical used to detect blood residue against presumably clean surfaces. He decided to scrub the kitchen down with a two-to-one mixture of bleach and water to remove as much trace evidence of the blood as possible. Fortunately, he already had what he needed at his disposal: six jugs of chlorine bleach, kept within easy reach of the shower for those frequent occasions when soap and water weren't enough to scrape away the filth.

When he was finished cleaning, he stared admirably at his work. With the exception of the dishes still piled in the sink, the kitchen hadn't looked so good in years. But even then, he was under no illusions that a crack team of CSI agents and blood splatter analysts wouldn't be able to find something, and so he resolved to tear out that revolting yellow linoleum and give the kitchen a badly needed makeover just as soon as possible.

Tomorrow would do. Or maybe the next day. It had been close to nine months since he'd been forced to resign from the office, and he figured it would be no skin off his ass to fit the floor job into his ritual of daily lawn mows and visits to the corner booze merchant. If anything, it would give him a good workout. Mix things up a bit.

Variety is the spice of life.

Parting the kitchen curtains, Henry spared one last look into the back yard where Vicky now lay under a three-foot layer of soil.

"Rot in peace," he said and poured himself a celebratory drink.

Thirty minutes and four bourbons later, Henry took the open jug of bleach into the bathroom and set it down on the toilet lid. He reached into the shower and cranked the knob to the hottest setting. Swaying drunkenly, he removed his clothes and placed them in the hamper.

From inside the medicine cabinet, he retrieved a handheld scrub brush. He raked it against his fingertips to ensure its bristles were firm as wafts of steam spilled from the shower stall, fogging his vision. He brought the brush and bleach with him under the scalding spray of water and scrubbed every inch of his body until his flesh screamed in agony.

When he lay his head against his pillow an hour later, he fell immediately into a dreamless sleep.

The next morning, Henry went into the back yard to take a look at his work by the light of day. To the untrained eye, there was nothing amiss. The garden had a freshly tilled look about it, but since he never allowed others onto his property there was no reason to believe anyone would notice a difference. For all the casual observer would know, it was just a square patch of earth where someone had once tried to plant radishes and tomatoes, its perimeter decorated by an askew platoon of foot-tall wooden garden gnomes that looked like some demented sculptor's creations frozen in time.

Henry eyed them with disdain. He wished he could destroy them. Just the thought got his adrenaline surging. But he was keenly aware that if he wanted to keep up appearances, he'd better not make significant changes to the décor anytime soon. Especially where the gnomes were concerned.

Every one of Vicky's friends knew of her love and fascination for the things, as surely as they knew of her desire to leave him and the fear she had of doing so. If any one of them had occasion to take notice her prized belongings had gone missing—expunged, like a chalkboard eraser wiping clean the slate of her existence—they'd know in a heartbeat something bad had happened to Vicky.

Premature celebrations had been the downfall of every lethal husband in recent history, all of them from that Jeffrey MacDonald guy all the way up to that Petersen idiot a few years back. Henry was damned if he was going to make the same mistake. It was decided. The garden gnomes would stay right where they were. For now.

Maybe I'll chop them up and use them for kindling in the winter. Give them each a slow, hot death. Wherever she is, I hope the bitch gets a front-row seat to that spectacle.

A wicked chuckle escaped his lips as he turned away from the garden. What he saw next melted the grin from his face and halted his motion like a baton to the belly. The periwinkle gnome—the one he'd kicked against the house last night; the one Vicky had called Perry—was staring out at him from behind the hedge just under the master bedroom window.

Henry blinked once. Hard. Then a second time, harder. His face knotted into a grimace when he did, then regained its shape as he stood allowing his eyes to focus on what he was fairly certain he was seeing.

It was Perry, alright. Not behind the hedge but actually planted inside of it, the top half of its torso extending upward from amid the dense shrubbery. Henry recognized it immediately from the color of its coat, but it was the splintered tip of the gnome's wooden head that left no doubt.

The force of the kick and the impact against the house had severed its triangular cap and left Perry with the appearance of a botched decapitation victim. All that remained was a single, horn-like spike that jutted out above the destroyed brow. Below it, two perfectly black, shark-like eyes gazed out.

Henry took a tentative step forward then stopped. He was almost certain the trajectory of Perry's flight had sent it in the opposite direction, but damned if he could remember now. Normally, it would have been easy for him to recall—aside from having an above average IQ, Henry also lay claim to a photographic memory that enabled him to capture, categorize, and instantly recall even the smallest of details—but the excitement of last night's events had screwed with his perceptions in a bad way and left his head buzzing with a state of euphoria he'd never experienced.

This must be what it's like to come down from a high, he thought. *No wonder junkies will do anything for their next fix. It chases away the paranoia.*

Closing the remaining distance to the hedge,

Henry reached out to pull the gnome from the shrubbery and felt a sharp, biting sting as its wooden teeth sank into the flesh of his outstretched hand.

Henry screamed. He reeled backward, nearly losing his footing, hugging his injured hand to his chest like a child who's just experienced his first encounter with a hot stove. He froze, staring at Perry with enormous, disbelieving eyes. He looked down at the palm of his hand. It was bleeding.

Did that just happen?

Perry stared at him from the perfectly maintained hedge, motionless.

That couldn't have just happened . . .

Henry dared a step forward. Then another. Finally, he saw it: a tiny, almost imperceptible splotch of red against the spike rising up from the gnome's wrecked skull.

All at once, the fear that had gripped him vanished and he breathed a sigh of relief so deep it felt like it was coming from the depths of his intestines. Henry laughed out loud. Old Perry's jagged head was apparently much worse than his bite.

I'm not losing my mind, he thought. *I've already lost it.*

Gingerly, so as not to accidentally wound himself again, he grasped the gnome by the neck and pulled it from the tightly woven shrub. He stared down at the grin carved into its elfish face.

"I'm going to burn you last," Henry swore, extending his arm in a sweeping gesture to indicate the dozen other garden gnomes positioned around the yard, "just so you can know what's coming."

It was insane, he knew, speaking aloud to an inanimate object. But then so was killing your wife and burying her in the back yard. Probably. Maybe. Who the hell cared?

He returned the gnome to the spot on the lawn it had occupied for god-knew-how-long and proceeded to pluck bloody splinters from his palm. The sight of blood had always had a centering effect on Henry. Even now. Even his own. It allowed his mind to focus, to contemplate those far-flung concepts and nebulous notions regular people often took for granted or somehow managed to completely ignore. Like how the hell an inanimate garden gnome could wind up ass-down in the shrubbery like a purposeful plant without having been deliberately placed there.

Had someone come into the yard last night? Maybe the next-door neighbor—that skinny little bastard with the ridiculous combover and seventies sideburns who always had a habit of running out to check his mail whenever he saw Vicky standing at the mailbox—had seen something go down through a knothole in the fence and had taken it upon himself to play detective? Or worse yet, troublemaker. Henry felt his heart skip a beat in his throat. For all he knew, Combover could be watching him this very moment.

In his mind's eye, he pictured the scenario unfolding: a gentle rap at the front door some late night, and a note left face-up on the porch reading, *I saw what you did. Deposit $50,000 electronically to the bank account below or I'll call the police.*

If that was the case, Vicky might be receiving company in her shallow grave sooner than the worms had had a chance to eat away her eyeballs.

Focusing all of his attention on his body

language like an actor on a stage, Henry took a casual, almost languid step in the direction of the fence that bordered Combover's property. Using his peripheral vision—a trick he'd taught himself long ago that enabled him to scope out the neighborhood teeny-boppers without coming off like one of those *To Catch a Predator* sickos— he watched the fence for signs of movement on the other side. When he was convinced there was no one there, he looked squarely in the direction of the neighbor's house.

Above the top edge of the fence between the drooping maple branches, he saw the drapes inside of Combover's home were drawn closed. Were they always closed like that? He tried to recall, but realized he'd never had occasion to make note of such an inconsequential detail. He was about to take another step closer when the phone inside the house began to ring.

Normally, he'd have let it go until Vicky picked up. Nobody ever called him anyway, and most of the time it was one of her friends, probably calling up to ask why she hadn't left him yet. He decided to let it ring—all the better to keep up appearances—but when it reached the ninth without letup, he figured he'd better answer.

Nice and easy, he coached himself. *Just like nothing happened.*

It was Vicky's sister, Lynne. He couldn't have been less displeased if it had been Vicky herself, phoning him up from the afterlife to harangue him for the indecency of not giving her a Christian burial.

"Is Vicky there?"

Lynne's tone was perfunctory. She might as well have been speaking to a hotel desk operator.

"No."

"Do you know where she is?"

Now there was something in Lynne's voice that was much more than the displeasure of having to speak to the man she'd spent the better part of the last ten years trying to convince her sister to leave. She sounded worried.

"I just got up," he said. "She's probably out shopping."

"We were supposed to meet this morning for breakfast." Now Lynne's voice seemed like it was straying close to panic. "She never showed up."

Henry glanced at the clock on the kitchen wall. 10:15 a.m. Vicky had been dead less than twelve hours. He hadn't counted on someone missing her just yet.

"I don't know where the hell she goes off to." He sounded irritated. It was what would have been expected of him, but he didn't have to fake the irritation. Then, for good measure, he added: "For all I care, she can stay gone."

When Lynne spoke next, her words came out in an almost pleading manner. There was no love lost between the estranged siblings-in-law, but at this moment it was more important to her to find out if her sister was okay.

"Can you at least check the garage to see if the car's still there?"

Henry snapped his eyes shut and opened them again. He hadn't thought about how he would explain his wife's sudden disappearance if one of her only lifelines to the outside world was still parked in the garage.

"Please?" Lynne added.

Henry ignored her phony courtesy.

Think fast.

Finally, he said, "Unless she suddenly decided

to get off her lazy ass and walk, she must have taken it."

I'm going to have to get rid of the damn car. Shit! And it's paid for.

He waited for Lynne to respond. She hung up on him instead.

"Bitch," he growled, then set the receiver back into its cradle and made himself breakfast.

The doorbell rang three hours later. It was the police.

Henry stared at the two uniformed officers—one of them a bleached blond beefcake with a perfect tan, the other the stereotype of an aging beat vet way past due for a desk job—with a perfectly bemused expression that indicated he had no idea what they were doing at his home.

"Can I help you?"

"Are you Henry Keller?" It was the beat vet, obviously in charge.

"I am."

"Can we come inside?"

Henry's first instinct was to refuse, but his

rational mind thought better. If he wanted to pass himself off as innocent, the worst thing he could do now was to behave uncooperatively.

"Of course," he said. "Come in."

Henry pushed the door open and moved aside, casually inserting his bandaged hand into the pocket of his sweatpants. Twenty years before, a killer nicknamed "OJ" had been fingered for his own wife's slaying based on a few unexplained cuts to the hand and a shaky alibi. Since Henry didn't have his very own Kato Kaelin to back up his lie, he knew he had to step cautiously.

"Mr. Keller, is your wife home?"

"No."

"Do you know where she is?"

"No. I woke up this morning and she was gone. I think she probably went out shopping, but I haven't heard from her. Why?"

"Have you tried calling her cell phone?"

"She doesn't have one," he replied, omitting the part about how he had refused to let her have one. "Neither of us do. It's too expensive. Why? What's going on? Did something happen to Vicky?"

Nice touch, he told himself. *You sound concerned.*

"We're responding to a missing persons report. Apparently, your wife hasn't been seen or heard from in over twenty-four hours."

Henry shook his head. "That's not true. She was home with me all day yesterday and we went to bed last night around ten."

The towheaded officer, the one with arms that looked like swollen calves, jotted something down in a pocket-sized notepad while the beat vet surveyed the immediate surroundings for signs of a disturbance. His glance drifted past Henry's shoulders and momentarily fixed on the kitchen linoleum before moving on.

So much for that floor job, Henry thought. *If they come back to find me playing Bob Fucking Vila, I'm screwed.*

It was just as well. It was an expense he couldn't have afforded, anyway.

"She's probably out buying a thousand things we'll never be able to pay off," Henry added, offering a helpless shrug that said it all: *Women!*

The beat vet cracked a knowing smile and nodded. Behind him, the beefcake cop stopped writing and grinned. "Same boat, different women."

Henry motioned to the kitchen. "Can I get you guys something? I don't have any coffee, but I make a hell of a cup of green tea."

They politely declined, as he suspected they would. After a few more questions, they left. Henry peered out from behind the living room vertical blinds and watched the squad car pull away.

Idiots didn't even ask if she'd taken the car. Keystone cops.

It didn't happen all at once. If it had, Henry might have been able to process the events more clearly in his head. Getting over the initial shock—that stubborn mental barrier that prevents people from accepting things for what they are and not what they *should* be—would have been enough of a challenge. But at least he wouldn't have been slowed by the worry that he was losing his mind. Instead, things began to happen at an almost imperceptible rate.

The first occurrence took place the night after

the police visit. He was in the kitchen, wiping down the linoleum again, when the giggling sounds began.

Goddamned kids.

Henry despised suburbia. He'd always figured himself far more suited to a metropolitan city life than amid the mindless breeders and Wal-Mart devotees of the world, but he bore the burden of his inability to afford a better lifestyle with admirable dignity. When it came to the neighborhood children, that dignity was often put to the test.

Since he couldn't very well lay a hand on them without legal consequences, he had opted to exercise his creativity by becoming an expert at blocking out the sights and sounds of what typically passed for a happy life among the plebeians of the world. The six-foot fence and maple trees had been a good start. But more often than not he found the best way to drown out the noise of his surroundings was simply by turning the knob of the kitchen radio to full volume.

It was another of those things Vicky had frequently protested against—reminding him that too much talk radio and not enough culture was bad for the soul, as well as the ears—but she'd never dared challenge him again after the gut-punch that had sent her sprawling on the very linoleum she would one day decorate with her blood.

And now the giggling. Mocking. As if intended solely for his ears.

Usually, the radio did the trick. But not tonight. It almost sounded like the kids were playing right outside his living room window.

Henry looked at the clock on the wall indicating it was quarter to ten.

Goddamned irresponsible parents.

He stood and marched to the front door. A few choice words for the little bastard noisemakers, loud enough for their parents to hear, would do the trick. But when he threw the door open there wasn't a soul in sight. The front lawn was empty, as was the sidewalk and the street beyond it. The only sound now was the audible hum of the overhead street lights.

The second he closed the door, he heard it again. This time the giggling seemed to be coming from someplace else. Somewhere much closer. Standing in his foyer with one hand still resting on the door knob, he turned his head like a slowly rotating antenna, zeroing in on the bearing of the disembodied snickers, and found himself staring at the grate of the heating duct only inches from his feet.

The giggling stopped. He didn't hear it again.

The second occurrence happened two days later. Lynne had called more than twenty times since. With each call, the tone of her voice became more desperate than it had been before. Henry took great pleasure in it, but finally decided to stop answering after she accused him of having done something terrible.

"I know you're hiding something," was all she got out before he hung up on her. When the phone rang again thirty seconds later, Henry put the ringer on mute and walked into the back yard where the lawnmower sat in wait under the light of a glorious summer afternoon.

The sun was high in the sky, and so was he. With Vicky dead and gone, there was no one left to break his balls about his drinking and he reveled in his newfound freedom by winding back the clock on Happy Hour a full ninety degrees. By noon, he was well on his way through his third vodka tonic.

Now that he'd had time to think things through, he decided to keep the car. Getting rid of it would only arouse suspicion. Besides, the Olds had been paid off for more than a year now and he'd be damned if he was going to take on a new car payment his unemployment wouldn't cover.

And so Henry had destroyed the contents of Vicky's purse—ID and credit cards included— and continued in the nightly ritual of scrubbing down the kitchen linoleum to a pristine polish. He eventually replaced the chlorine bleach with oxygen bleach, which his meticulous research had shown to be far more effective at throwing forensics experts for a loop.

Not that he felt he had anything to worry about. With the first forty-eight hours officially timed out, he was more confident than ever that the police would find no reason to suspect he'd done anything wrong.

And if they knew Vicky, he thought, *they might even think I'd done something very right.*

They'd been back again, of course. Additional follow-up questions, this time from an entirely new set of faces, even a request to pay a visit downtown to make an official statement, to which he'd acquiesced graciously. Henry had impressed himself with his Oscar-worthy portrayal of fear-stricken, worry-laden husband. At one point he'd even broken down in crocodile tears when asked if it was possible his wife had left him for another man.

Henry was studied in the art of deception; he knew that people who made false statements invariably cast their eyes away when they did, and so he made it a point to look straight into the eyes of every uniform who questioned him. But not for too long. Eye contact was generally believed to be an indicator of honesty, but prolonged eye contact was often thought to be a sign of intentional lying.

Taking his performance to an altogether professional level, he had even gone so far as to call twice a day to speak to the investigator in charge to ask for updates, offering up inane suggestions that amounted to no more than red herrings: "The last time we spoke, she talked about visiting her mother's grave in Pittsburgh—have you checked with hotels in that area?"

Once, he even suggested the police thumb through Vicky's old high school yearbooks for names and phone numbers of men she might still be in contact with—all in the hopes of uncovering some kernel that would lead them to where she'd gone.

"If she's left me for someone else," he told them, "I don't hold it against her. I've never been the most attentive husband. But I just need to know she's okay."

By the fourth day, the police station receptionist stopped putting his calls through to the investigator in charge.

Mission accomplished.

Out in the back yard, fifteen feet from Vicky's rotting corpse, Henry kicked the lawnmower to life. He hadn't cut the grass since the morning of the murder, and even though he knew the uncharacteristically unkempt appearance of his lawn only served to paint him as the despondent husband letting his life go straight to hell, he simply couldn't bear to look at it any longer. Murdering your wife was one thing. Allowing your surroundings to devolve into utter chaos was a crime deserving of capital punishment.

As he mowed, he kept one eye trained on Combover's house. So far, no notes had been left on Henry's porch. There had been no mysterious phone calls, no unusual activity at all to indicate the sickly, saggy-fleshed bastard next door would present himself as a problem.

Yet when Henry thought about the purposeful position in which he'd discovered Perry the day after the dirty deed, he could surmise only two possible scenarios: either the garden gnome had landed that way on its own (which he still wasn't entirely convinced was possible) or it had been put there. If it was the latter, Henry thought, he might have to deal with that situation sooner rather than later.

You always wanted to get closer to my wife. Maybe now you'll have your chance. I could climb over the fence one night. From there, it would be a cakewalk to pry open a back window and—

The lawnmower struck something. From the

corner of his eye, Henry saw a flash of movement. He whipped his head forward to find one of the garden gnomes lying directly in the path of the mower.

Not Perry—not this time. This was one of the others. The one with the crimson-colored coat pushing a dark green wheelbarrow Vicky had so unimaginatively christened "Red." For a moment, Henry thought he had been so preoccupied plotting Combover's demise that he'd accidentally veered the mower off course. It wasn't until he killed the motor and checked the perfectly straight mow-line behind him that he observed Red had fallen out of formation by at least five feet.

Keeping the gnome in his sight the whole time, Henry walked around to the front of the lawnmower and shoved Red away with his foot, recoiling at the last second like an arachnophobe stomping out a lethal threat. It cartwheeled in the grass and came to rest on its side just inches from where it had been all along. The thing's eyes glared at him accusingly as if to say, "You'll pay for that."

Two houses away, the yapper that had graced

the neighborhood with silence for the last half hour began its tirade again. The noise snapped Henry back to reality with the force of a tap to the balls. He looked over his shoulder to see the curtains inside of Combover's home had been pulled open.

He's watching me, Henry thought, and a sudden rush of fury tinted everything in his perspective a dark violet. *I don't know how the hell that son of a bitch did it or what game he's playing, but it ends tonight.*

Not bothering to roll the lawnmower back inside the shed, Henry retreated into the house. Maybe another vodka tonic—heavy on the former, easy on the latter—would settle his nerves. He had some more killing to do.

The yapper was at it again. Its owners, oblivious. That suited Henry just fine. Tonight, he was glad for the diversion. It would make getting over the fence and into Combover's home unheard that much easier.

He waited until after midnight. He would have preferred to take care of business by light of day (the thought of having to walk past Vicky's gnomes in the dark of a moonless night made his scrotum tingle unpleasantly) but he couldn't risk anyone seeing him climb the fence. He also knew he couldn't wait for Combover to make the first move. If the guy hadn't already gone to the police, it was just a matter of time before he did.

Henry let himself out of the house and crossed the lawn, forming a wide arc around the gnomes. In his imagination, he could envision feeling their small wooden hands taking hold of the hem of his pants, all of them at once, bringing him down in a roiling pile of flesh and lumber. He fought the urge to run past them, but by the time he reached the shed he was almost trotting.

Without flipping the light switch, Henry reached inside the shed and retrieved the small step-ladder from its designated place beside the door. The fact he needed no light to locate it gave him a sense of pride. If more men kept their wives in line and their sheds in order, he believed, the world would be a far better place to inhabit.

He brought the ladder outside and propped it gently against the fence post where the drooping maple branches nearly scraped the tops of the slats. Stepping lightly, he lifted himself up and peeked across.

Complete darkness engulfed the neighbor's yard. The only light on inside the house was the glow of a TV set in one of the bedrooms where he presumed Combover lay, sleeping or near-asleep, probably watching some reality show where contestants degraded themselves for their promised fifteen minutes of shame.

Two houses down, the yapper paused briefly to catch its breath. When it began its discordant night song again, Henry pulled himself up and was over the fence in one swift motion.

Now all that was left to do was to get inside. The meat hammer he had cleaned to a meticulous shine and stuck into his back pocket would do the rest. He had no fear that Combover would put up much of a struggle. As it was, the guy looked like a washed-out relic from another era just waiting for someone to put an end to his misery. Henry was more than happy to oblige.

Luck struck once when he tried the back door and found it unlocked. Then a second time when he came upon the bedroom of the single-level home to find Combover fast asleep on his back. One hand was cradling the remote control; the other was tucked into the waistband of his jockeys.

In the distance, the yapper woofed and wailed. If only its owners knew their disregard would be responsible for masking discovery of tonight's devilish deed, they might have shot the dog and themselves out of pure shame. Henry drew the meat hammer from his back pocket, raised his arm over his head, and swung with all his might.

The first blow hit Combover in the crotch, shattering the bones of his hand and pulverizing the organ in its embrace. An agonized gasp escaped his mouth and he lay convulsing, eyes bulged open, struggling to catch his breath like an asthmatic in the throes of a final attack.

Henry didn't wait for Combover to gain the breath necessary to scream. He pounced on him like an animal to the kill, pummeling him viciously with the meat hammer, over and over, until even his involuntary death spasms had ceased.

When he finally caught his breath and his heart rate at last found its natural rhythm, Henry looked around him. The walls of the tiny bedroom were splattered with blood. Even the TV screen was covered with it, casting the room in a hellish crimson glow. On the bed below him, Combover lay dead—his head flattened to a grotesque pulp.

Combover would do no talking to the police. And if he already had? At least Henry could take comfort in knowing he'd delivered payback with extreme interest.

In the bathroom, Henry removed every strip of clothing and shoved it all into the plastic bag he'd stuffed into his hip pocket. He threw the meat hammer in there, as well. Then he stepped into his victim's shower and rinsed the blood and bits of brain from his body.

As the cool light of clarity descended upon him, Henry realized it would be impossible to move Combover into Vicky's grave. Even if he could get him over the fence without leaving a bloody trail in his wake, the mess in the bedroom could never be cleaned without setting a match to the place.

They'll never put the pieces together, he assured himself. *Besides, it'll probably be a month or two before anybody finds the mess.*

After he'd dried himself off, he exited naked through the back door into the yard, taking the plastic bag with him, and hopped over the fence again.

People get caught doing this shit? Amateurs.

He rejoiced in the freedom his nakedness brought. He could have howled into the night to match the yapper's still-resonating screams, but he was aware of his senses enough to hold himself in reserve. Moving calmly, almost serenely, he returned the ladder to the shed and set the gore-soaked plastic bag into an empty cardboard box underneath the workbench.

Once outside, he padlocked the shed door and stood breathing in the warm, fresh night air. He felt he could have stood that way all night until the dawn, eyes closed, face upturned to the sky, but the weight of his responsibilities—the need to wash the soil from between his toes, the call of the bristle brush and bleach in his own shower—tugged him from his reverie.

Henry opened his eyes to see the garden gnomes had formed a circle around him.

Not just Perry this time, or Red.

The whole goddamned army.

Before, it had been easy enough to rationalize away. Even if someone hadn't been playing a trick on him, it was possible that Perry had landed in the shrubbery by dumb luck. Maybe even probable that Henry had somehow knocked Red out of formation while setting up the lawnmower and simply not noticed. But this . . .

The frightening skip in his heartbeat returned. This time he felt it in his temples. A dizzying sensation racked him and for the briefest moment, Henry felt he could have passed out right there on the lawn.

If it wasn't for the fear of what might become of him if he did—of what the garden gnomes would do to him—he might have. But in the last moments before consciousness left him, something struck to life inside of Henry and he bolted into motion, vaulting the blockade of foot-tall gnomes, racing for the house like a man with the devil on his ass.

Had he screamed, or made any sound at all, he might have spared himself the terror of what he heard as he slammed the sliding glass door closed behind him: the sound of two dozen tiny footsteps padding after him across the lawn.

He didn't step foot outside the house for another three days.

Henry Keller never placed much stock in dreams. He considered them little more than psychological regurgitations of past experience, and always held a mocking laugh for those who suggested the possibility that dreams could ever act as portents of things to come. But as the days wore on and the dreams of the garden gnomes persisted, he found himself questioning that certainty. Just as he began to question the existence of the line between reality and non-reality.

One week after Vicky's death—right around the time the worms would have finished feasting on what little remained of her brain, he presumed—the dreams began. They were unlike any he'd ever had before, with a vividness and clarity that made waking life seem dreamlike in comparison.

In one of them, the garden gnomes crept into his room as he lay sleeping and pinned him underneath the bed sheet while Perry drove the splintered tip of his skull into Henry's stomach. In another, it was Vicky herself who showed up at the foot of his bed, the pungent odor of rotting flesh accompanying her arrival, the pupils of her eyes replaced by a pink, milky substance that leaked down her face and splattered onto the carpet with sickening plops.

"You did this to me," she cried in an inhuman rasp. "You bastard, *you* did this to me!"

Henry had woken up screaming every time, the sound of his own voice terrifying him more than the dreams.

But it wasn't until the night Combover came to him—lying beside him like a lover and rubbing his flabby flesh against Henry's back—that he finally woke with the determination to rid himself of the gnomes once and for all.

It's all their doing, he rationalized. *All their fault. Once they're gone, the dreams will follow.*

Sitting up in bed, he looked at the bedside clock. 3:15 a.m. As good a time as any. If he was going to do this, he had better do it now. He pulled on his robe and went into the back yard.

The moon was out, offering just enough illumination to reveal the platoon of garden gnomes standing in broken formation around Vicky's grave like sentinels. Henry picked up the galvanized steel trash can he kept next to the back door and brought it into the middle of the yard.

He didn't allow himself to think. If he had, he could never have worked up the nerve to touch the gnomes with his bare hands, even if just long enough to scoop them up and drop them into the trash can like hot coals. But a sense of urgency had taken over—the same sense of urgency that told him if he didn't get rid of the gnomes right away, the dreams would drive him mad—and he leaped into action, working his way methodically through their ranks, filling the trash can with their bodies, until only two remained: Red and Perry, who stood with their bodies turned toward one another as if caught mid-conversation.

"Sorry to interrupt," Henry heard himself say, "but your lease is up."

The sheer madness—the outright ludicrousness—of addressing them like sentient beings was not lost on him. Yet at the same time he felt strangely *normal* doing so. As if some sliver of subconscious awareness told him they understood every word, despite their inability to reply.

"It's trash day today." Henry set his hands on his hips as if to emphasize the significance of his pronouncement. "That means in just a few hours, you and all your merry friends will be neck-deep in shitty diapers and rotting mac 'n cheese out at the county landfill."

Just the thought drew a smile on his face. All of the wasted, painstaking hours Vicky had put into their care, those blistering summer days spent tending to their sun-faded coats with paintbrush in hand in her attempts to preserve them in all their original garish splendor, would now amount to nothing.

As much as Henry had relished the idea of holding an all-out bonfire with the garden gnomes as the sacrificial guests of honor, their end would not come by flame. Getting rid of them this early in the game was enough of a gamble. Destroying them in such a conspicuous manner would simply provoke too much suspicion. And there was no way in hell he was keeping them around until winter, until things had died down enough for the sight of smoke billowing from the upturned snout of his chimney to appear perfectly within the realm of the ordinary. No. It had to be done with. Tonight.

He leaned over and picked Red up by the wheelbarrow. Even in his freshly emboldened state, he still wanted nothing to do with actually touching the things if he could help it. Quickly, he dropped Red into the trash on top of the others. Then he turned his attention to Perry. Vicky's *precious*. Its misshapen head pointed skyward like a miniature-scale impaling stake. Its cheerful, beard-framed grin belied the black intent of its eyes.

Slowly, cautiously, Henry closed his fingers

around the garden gnome's waist. His eyelids twitched and the muscles of his back stiffened in anticipation of what he feared might come. When nothing did, he tossed Perry into the trash can and fastened the lid firmly into place. Then he dragged the can around the side of the house and set it down on the front curb.

He picked up one of the cinderblock stepping stones that led from the driveway to the front porch and placed it on top of the garbage can lid.

"Just in case I'm not stark raving mad," he muttered under his breath, then went inside and collapsed into bed.

He couldn't remember the last time he'd slept so long. Almost fourteen hours, according to the digital readout that stared back at him when he finally woke at 5:05 p.m. the following afternoon. The sleep had done him well. He hadn't felt this good in years.

Recalling the nightmares that had plagued him for the past week, Henry rifled his brain for anything—any memory, even the vaguest recollection or fragment of a dream—and relaxed satisfactorily against his pillow at the perfectly blank slate that stared back at him.

Gone. Just like Vicky. Just like Combover. Just like those goddamned gnomes.

An urgent knocking at the front door pulled Henry to full consciousness.

Standing slowly, he steadied himself like a drunk rising for the first time after a two-day bender. Too much time on your back may have been good for the body, but it played hell on the equilibrium. By the time he made it to the front door, the knocking had grown insistent.

He might have laughed at the constipated looks on the faces of the two police officers— Beefcake and Beat Vet, the same incompetents who had shown up on his doorstep the morning after Vicky's death—had it not been for the shrewd sense of caution that even now informed his every outward expression. Henry knew the reason they were here. It was only a matter of time before someone noticed Combover had gone missing. Or caught the stench radiating from the walls of his home.

"Mr. Keller, have you heard from your wife?"

This time it was Beefcake doing the talking.

They must take turns at this, he thought.

"No." Henry allowed his face to drop and his shoulders to wilt almost (but not quite) imperceptibly before going on. "And the sergeant in charge has stopped taking my calls." Then, painting his face with an insincere dash of hopeful optimism, he added: "Did you find anything yet?"

The two officers exchanged a look. Beefcake looked away impatiently as Beat Vet took up the slack.

"Nothing, sorry."

Far beneath the veneer of concern, Henry studied them. The last time these two jokers had shown up, there had been an almost apologetic manner about them. Not today. Today, they were all business.

Beat Vet wasted no time. "Do you know Melvyn Toms?"

"No."

"The neighbor just south of your property."

Combover.

"No," Henry repeated. "I pretty much keep to myself."

"Mr. Toms was found dead in his home."

Henry feigned surprise. "Oh?"

"Murdered."

Now Henry could sense with almost animalistic awareness that the cops weren't just here to ask questions. They were probing.

"Oh," he said again, this time infusing his pronunciation of the word with something that almost resembled concern. "That's awful."

Beefcake regarded him with a steely gaze. His head was cocked at an odd angle, reminding Henry of a dog trying to perceive something just outside of its ability to do so. Beat wore the expression of an idiot struggling to make sense of an incomprehensible math equation. He pitied them both. When neither spoke, Henry decided to put an end to the uncomfortable silence himself.

"Does this have something to do with my wife?"

Beat shifted his weight uncomfortably and ignored the question. "We'd like the opportunity to have a quick look in your back yard," he said. When Henry didn't respond, he added, "With your permission."

A single bead of sweat trickled from Henry's forehead and ran down the length of his nose. It hung from the tip of his nostril for an impossibly long moment, as if somehow exempted from the pull of gravity, before finally dropping onto his upper lip.

The police asking permission to have "a quick look" in his back yard was tantamount to asking if it was okay for them to set up permanent residence in his living room until they'd found something to tie him to Vicky and Combover. And there was no way he could afford to let that happen.

Not a chance in hell.

Henry considered his options. He could try fooling them with tears of insincerity again. To this point, they'd all bought into his bullshit like suckers at an auction. But now he was coming to the realization that that hunting dog was overdue for its appointment with the euthanasist. He thought about faking a grand mal seizure, possibly putting off giving his permission until after they'd taken him to the ER, but Henry had never been much for delaying the inevitable. He even considered dredging up a serving of phony indignation in response to their unspoken accusation. But the fact was, he had grown bored of the game. Instead, Henry looked Beat straight in the eye and said, "I'd rather not."

For an instant, both officers looked stunned. And then a dim light of understanding began to register in their eyes. It was all that either man needed to understand exactly what had gone on.

"At this point it's probably in your best interests to cooperate," Beefcake tried, but his voice trailed away into silence.

Henry's face had drawn completely blank. The mask of emotion he'd donned so effortlessly during his interactions with the bastards in blue was gone. All that stared out now reflected cold cunning. When he spoke again, his voice was dark.

"Do you have a warrant?"

Beefcake and Beat glanced at one another in unspoken comprehension.

"No," Beat said, "but that can be arranged."

Henry wiped at the pool of sweat on his upper lip, suddenly aware that he was drenched again. Just like he had been the night he'd killed Vicky with the meat tenderizer. Just like the night he'd pounced on Combover as he lay dreaming whatever perverted dreams such dreamers dreamt. If the sons of bitches before him weren't armed, he'd have done the same to them.

"Then you'd better go arrange it," he told them.

♥.●.♪♪♪

He figured he had about two hours before they came back. He had to get rid of Vicky's body. Now.

Cut her into pieces and flush her down the toilet?
No.
Throw her into the trunk of the Olds and drop what's left of her in a dumpster somewhere?

It could work. It had almost worked for that Hacking guy in Utah. But even without a body, the authorities could still press charges. He knew he couldn't very well let them find her on their own. He had to do something.

Henry peered out the kitchen window and stared up at the multi-colored halo of strobing police lights spewing upward from the street in front of Combover's house. All that separated him from the investigation taking place there was the fence between back yards. A wave of desperation swept him as he realized he would never be able to move Vicky's body. Not now. Not with a battalion of police within spying distance.

I have to get the hell out of here.

Up to that moment, he'd never considered the possibility of running. But once the idea was introduced to his conscious mind, Henry saw it was the only remaining course of action that made any sense.

Without a thought as to where he would go or what he'd do when he got there, he picked up the key ring from the kitchen counter and started for the garage. Only the sudden recollection of the plastic sack he'd stuck into the cardboard box inside the shed—the sack containing the murder weapon and the bloody clothes he'd worn into Combover's home—stopped him.

If he left it behind, it would only be a matter of minutes before the police found it.

They'll have an APB out for me from here to the state line, he thought.

But if he took it with him and got rid of it, he

could get a head start on them.

Five, maybe ten hours at most before they decide to start digging and discover Vicky's body.

For the last time in his life, Henry pulled open the sliding glass door and passed through the threshold into his back yard. The sky overhead was darkening to a deep purple hue, but the police lights continued their dance, projecting against the bruise-colored backdrop like a low-rent light show.

He figured if he moved quickly he could get in and out of the shed unseen, and so he began to walk, eyes fixed on the fence, watching for any activity beyond it, fingers fumbling for the padlock key as he stepped around the phalanx of garden gnomes in his path. When he got to the shed, he slid the key into the padlock and removed it. He tossed the lock into the grass and reached inside. As his fingers closed around the light switch, he stopped.

What happened next took place in the span of a millisecond. As Henry stared into the darkness, the afterimage of something caught in his peripheral vision—the sight of the gnomes, standing in formation in the yard again—

replayed itself against the cold, dark space before him like a visual stutter. Simultaneously, the subconscious recollection of a noise much like the sound of trash cans being knocked over in the early hours of the morning bubbled to the surface.

The gnomes . . . ?

Before he had a chance to process the thought, a lightning bolt of blinding pain shot up his calf from the tip of his right foot. He kicked his leg instinctively and heard something crash against the exterior wall of the shed. Something wooden. He jerked his head in the direction of the noise and saw one the garden gnomes resting motionless on the ground, its body split into two clean pieces from the impact.

Bewildered, Henry stared at the fractured, unmoving corpse.

Impossible, he thought, but no sooner had the word crystallized in his mind than the intense throbbing pain in his foot superseded the insistent denial, calling him back to reality from a thousand miles away. He looked down and saw the shoe of his right foot had been torn open at the toe, exposing a matted, bloody mess.

What the hell?

His heart was racing again. This time it pounded in his ears with the strength of a jackhammer. He bent over to inspect the injury, reaching out for it with trembling fingers before drawing his hand back suddenly, as if deciding he didn't want to know the extent of the damage. Not yet. Not until he figured out what the hell was going on. His eyes darted back to the still, broken gnome.

Did that thing do this to me? But, how?

There was a crawling sensation on the back of his neck now. Not quite like the feeling of being watched. More like the sense of being approached.

Resting the full weight of his body on his left foot, Henry pivoted slowly and turned to face the horde of garden gnomes. Somehow, they had made it out of the trash can on the street and into the back yard again. And somehow, they were moving.

The realization struck him like a full tilt sensory assault, powerful enough to drive his attention away from the pain radiating upward from his shattered toe. In the moments before they attacked, in the fading light of the blackening sky, Henry saw them closing in.

Their small wooden bodies moved in impossibly jerky motions that called to mind all those ridiculous stop-motion Sinbad movies he'd seen as a child—the ones that depicted flying demons and walking skeletons doing battle against bare-chested, bearded heroes in loin cloths—only there was something far more incredible about what he was witnessing now.

The gnomes hadn't come to life. Not exactly. Not in the *proper* sense, and certainly not the way he had envisioned they might, even in his most terrifying nightmares. In the dreams, they had moved about with an almost cartoonish fluidity, lighting from one spot to the next with unnatural ease. But the reality of what he was seeing was far more inconceivable than that. As if the veil that separated the living from the inanimate had been abruptly torn away, imbuing their once immobile joints with just enough flex to allow them to move of their own volition.

Even their paraphernalia—the walking sticks they used to hold themselves upright, the smoking pipes that dangled from their bearded jaws, the tiny lanterns slung over their shoulders with orange glowing cores—had somehow come alive with them. They breathed in a hive-like, unified pulse.

Henry had only enough time for one thought to race through his head.

This can't be happening.

And then they were upon him.

They closed the distance fast, their approach accentuated by the staccato rhythm of their tiny wooden feet drumming across the lawn. Six of them crashed against his ankles, clawing through the fabric of his pants, latching their talon-like fingertips into his flesh like fishhooks. One of them sank piranha-like teeth into the tendons of his heel, drawing blood. Another used the small wooden pickaxe carved into its grip to hammer at his ankle bone.

The pain was nothing compared to the horror of their touch. A long-buried memory of Uncle Albert, pouncing on him as he lay sleeping in his underwear in his childhood bed, exploded to the surface like a dislodged submersible buoy and Henry heard himself cry out. It seemed to come from someplace far above him. Removed.

Distant. Unfamiliar.

Then came the second wave of gnomes, thrusting their weight against the first, their bodies clattering loudly as they heaved forward in an attempt to throw Henry off balance and drive him down. Only the shed itself prevented him from falling, and he let out an astonished cry as his spine collided with the doorjamb and split the back of his shirt down the middle. His head snapped backward and struck the aluminum siding with an almost comical, exclamatory pop.

Kicking wildly, he managed to stay on his feet—but the stars that spun and danced in his field of vision made it impossible for him to see what was coming next. He began to swing his arms furiously, striking nothing, legs now beginning to strain under the impossibly heavy weight of the gnomes that piled over one another in their attempts to scale him.

He could feel them making their way up his body, inflicting as much damage as they could in their ascent. One of them paused just below his waist and pummeled mercilessly at his crotch before continuing upward. Another plunged what felt like a hot poker into the flesh just below his left nipple. Henry clutched at his breast and screamed in agony as tiny pincers closed around his fingertips, leaving them bloody stumps.

Matchstick-like claws raked against his neck as the first of the gnomes reached his upper torso and straddled his shoulder. There was the faint, hideous sensation of breath against his ear as it unfurled its jaw and closed its mouth around his earlobe, rending it loose in a spray of blood.

Henry got out one final, desperate scream—a cry of intermingled outrage and terror—but the gnome that launched its head into the cavity of his mouth silenced him. His eyes bulged and his entire head seemed almost to expand as the creature burrowed its solid, unyielding body deeper in, snapping viciously at Henry's tongue, tearing at his gums, stabbing at his throat, finally plunging the tip of its splintered head directly into his exposed windpipe.

In an instant, Henry's bodily instincts were tripped. An uncanny cool descended over him and his vision cleared to eagle-like clarity as the panic receded and was replaced at once with a singular physical imperative. He bent himself in half at the waist and stretched his neck forward, somehow managing to wrap his hands around the knees of the wooden creature trying to tunnel its way down his throat. In one violent motion, he tore it out. It came easily, bringing the front half of his tongue with it.

Arms extended at full length, Henry held the creature in his grip like a doomed adventurer regarding some strange and terrifying discovery. He gaped in dismay as the garden gnome swallowed what remained of his tongue and fixed him with a smug, defiant scowl.

It was Perry.

The entire upper half of the gnome's body was coated with a phlegmy substance Henry presumed to be the insides of his larynx. Large chunks of bloody flesh clung to the sharp tip of Perry's head and hung down like limp rabbit ears. The gnome's face, which had once worn the semblance of a fat man's jovial grin, had transformed into a demonic sneer. Its eyes, formerly black pinpricks against a flesh-colored coat of paint, now swam with a palpable depth.

Henry tried to scream, but all that came was a hoarse gurgle. With all of his strength, he pitched the gnome away from him like a fastball. Perry tumbled end over end in the air and landed in the grass with a dull thump. Three of the gnomes that had attached themselves to Henry's throwing arm also went with it, but the moment they landed they sprung immediately to their feet and began charging back across the lawn toward him.

The time it took for them to reach him gave him enough of a head start. Henry began to flail violently, like an animal in a trap, sending the other gnomes flying away from him two and three at a time. One of them struck the side of the house and broke into pieces. Another landed in the shrubbery face-first, its legs kicking like pistons as it tried to extricate itself.

Throwing himself backward against the shed, Henry managed to free himself from another which had torn a hole into the seat of his pants and was trying with all its might to shove its walking stick through the fabric of his underwear. The final two, their tiny timber fists gripping the hairline at the base of his neck, flew away as Henry tucked himself into a somersault and rolled savagely forward.

Something cracked on impact and he felt his right arm go numb. Thirty years earlier he might have been able to pull off that acrobatic move with only bruises to show, but that was then and this was now, and at this moment a dislocated arm was the least of Henry's concerns. Lying flat on his back, he raised his head to see the remaining gnomes forming a close circle around him.

At the head of the congregation stood Perry, a grotesque likeness of his former periwinkle self, glazed in crimson gore. The rest of the gnomes gathered around behind Perry as willing soldiers in a battle to the death, their formerly mirthful faces contorted into fierce war masks. Their tiny, splinter-like teeth gnashed together as their voices—*Dear god, their voices!*—coalesced into an inhuman chant.

Blood pulsed from Henry's mouth as he forced himself into a sitting position. Mercifully, there was no pain now. Only the incessant hammering of his heart against his temples, and a single, urgent thought.

The shed . . . the shed! Get inside the shed!

Gathering every ounce of strength left in his

body, Henry pulled himself to his feet, staggered backward into the shed, and closed himself in.

Outside, dusk was in full descent.

Henry lay in a pool of his own blood and wondered how long he had left to live. Bitterly, he wished Beat Vet and Beefcake would hurry up with their warrant already, but he knew they would never arrive in time. And if they did? They'd likely rush him to the hospital in their efforts to save his life, only to do their damnedest to send him to the gas chamber the moment he was well enough to walk upright on his own.

Over, Henry thought. *I'm over.*

If he'd had a gun, he would have used it on himself. Never mind the garden gnomes that even now continued in their tireless efforts to get to him, throwing themselves against the shed door, trying in vain to tunnel underneath the walls, even using one another as makeshift battering rams to pierce the walls of the shed. He knew they would never get in, just as surely as he knew he would never get out. Not alive.

Through the crack between the shed door and the jamb, he could see their shadows moving in the dark. Between attacks, they retreated and huddled into small groups. He thought he could hear whispers but could make out no words or even the faintest hint of a discernible language. What did it matter, anyway? He had nothing to say to them—couldn't if he wanted to—and he was pretty certain they had nothing to say to him. All that was left to do now was to wait for death.

The gnome on the workbench in the garage had been his undoing. Henry realized this now as the strength drained from his limbs and the life seeped from his wounds in deep red, oily rivulets. He had forgotten all about it—the gnome with the faded coat Vicky had brought into the garage to repaint the day before her death.

In his imagination, Henry pictured the thing stirring to life through whatever unknowable force that had awakened the others. Climbing from the workbench. Exiting the garage through the window overlooking the rose bushes. Toppling the trash can to release its imprisoned brethren. Even now he could sense its presence, standing only feet away on the other side of the barricade of plywood and cheap siding, the catalyst that had gifted Vicky the last word in their final life-and-death quarrel.

He tried to call out for help but found himself too weak to utter any more than a wounded whimper. Forcing his eyes open, Henry looked up and saw Vicky standing before him. Or what was left of her. Two purple, veiny hands held the soil-matted comforter around her like a burial shroud. Her eyes were gone. In their place, black sockets ringed with the decayed remains of her eyelids seemed to search for him. The flesh of her face was leathery. Her jaw quavered like a trap door on failing hinges and fresh dirt spilled from her mouth when she spoke.

"Surprise, my love," he heard her say, and when she spoke her voice had a strangely earthy, peaceful quality about it that she'd never had in life. It was the voice of the dead.

"Come die with me," she implored. "Come and die, Henry."

Unconsciousness began to wash over him. He gave himself to it willingly, drifting deeper into its embrace, certain he wanted nothing to do with what was waiting for him on the other side of it—*Vicky? Purgatory? Hell itself?*—yet too defeated to fight its pull.

Blackness swallowed him. Then silence.

It was the smell of smoke that pulled him back. Coming from just outside the shed.

Henry sat upright, nostrils flared, not nearly as dead as he'd presumed himself to be. Propping himself up with his uninjured arm, he peeked through the narrow slit that separated him from what lay in wait outside.

The garden gnomes were building a fire. Using the corpses of their fallen as kindling and the smoldering tips of their pipes to set the bodies alight, they began to kick the small flaming bundles toward the shed.

Henry pursed his lips together and watched helplessly. Blood pooled inside his lower lip and oozed out the sides of his mouth.

The first of the tinder rolled only a foot before extinguishing itself in the grass. The second managed to make it all the way to the exterior wall of the shed, but it failed to ignite and eventually petered out in a curling finger of smoke.

Laughter began to choke its way up Henry's lungs. It ended abruptly when the temperature inside the shed rose sharply.

No . . .

An inhuman grunt burst from his mouth, which no longer looked like a mouth as much as it did a swollen, puckered orifice. He tried to stand and fell face-first against the door, breaking his nose. A shockwave of searing heat pressed inward from the other side, singeing his eyelashes and blistering his forehead.

No!

Thrashing, Henry somehow regained his balance and lurched to his feet.

They won't burn me alive!

He pressed a hand against the door and lunged backward as a white-hot current coursed through his body from his charred fingertips.

I won't die like this! Not this way . . .

He shoved against the door with his shoulder, determined now to face them head-on—*I'd rather die fighting! Let me die fighting*—but the door refused to budge. He tried again, this time hurling his full weight against it. Nothing.

Sacrificing themselves, four of the remaining garden gnomes had wedged their pointed heads underneath the shed door to prevent it from opening. Their small bodies sent up plumes of white smoke as the flames devoured them.

Inside the shed, Henry let out a horrific screech as the heat of the fire melted his pants to the flesh of his legs. Chunks of flame rained down on his head, lighting his hair on fire as the roof of the shed ignited and began to collapse.

He kicked and screamed and thrashed and convulsed, but it wasn't long before everything within the shed—Henry included—was consumed.

It was not a merciful death.

By the time the fire department arrived, the inferno had burned itself out. Beat Vet and Beefcake arrived on the scene shortly after the police officers next door spotted the blaze and called in the firefighters. What they witnessed was quite possibly the most bizarre confessional either would ever behold.

The equipment shed on Henry Keller's property had burned to the ground in an apparent suicide. Embedded in the remaining framework of the structure lay a handful of charred wooden figures that had presumably been used as incendiary. A pile of smoldering ash was all that remained of the property's former resident.

Feet away from the grisly scene, a small patch of soil had been unearthed to reveal an even more ghastly discovery: the decaying corpse of a female, lying atop what appeared to be an unfurled comforter. Her arms had been crossed over her chest in a traditional burial pose.

Situated at precise intervals, forming a perfect circle around the uncovered grave, stood an odd assemblage of wooden garden gnomes, their jolly expressions offering stark contrast to the carnage on display. Not a living soul paid notice to the fact their wooden fingertips were caked in soil.

ABOUT THE AUTHOR

Vince Font is a fulltime writer and editor with a passion for B-movies and bacon. He shares living quarters with his wife and two fur babies and prides himself on being a better writer than half of his household occupants. His first book, *American Sons: The Untold Story of the Falcon and the Snowman,* was published in 2013. He is the founder and chief editor of Glass Spider Publishing, a hybrid micropublisher in Ogden, Utah. Visit www.glassspiderpublishing.com to learn more.